The Adventures
Binky, Banky and

Acknowledgements

Thank you to my daughter Jill for encouraging me to write down the tales of the three little monkeys. It would not have happened without her.

Thank you to my son-in-law Doccy for typing out the handwritten stories.

Thank you To James Kelly for being a mentor to Jill and for guiding her in publishing this series.

The Adventures of Binky, Banky and Bonky

Created and written by
George Bradley

Illustrated by
Ghulam Muhammed

ISBN: 978-1-7397731-0-6
Copyright © 2022

Book #1 in the series.

www.bbbpublishing.com

In Africa, parts of the rainforests were being destroyed. Trees were being cut down for logging to make furniture and build homes. Monkeys, who had lived very happily in the treetops, tried to escape further into the rainforest.

A few of the younger monkeys were caught by hunters who sold them in the local markets for pets. Three of these monkeys were bought by an animal charity and sent to a zoo in England.

This zoo was managed by
Mr. Popplethwaite. He was a
very kind and jolly man
with grey hair and a
round tummy.

When Mr. Popplethwaite found out that three monkeys were being sent to his zoo, he immediately made plans to build a nice comfortable place for them to live. The small house was built next to an oak tree and the zookeepers piled lots of straw on the floor to keep the monkeys warm.

In one corner of the enclosure, workers placed four tall tree trunks and added ropes and a tyre to give the monkeys a great place to climb and play. An old see-saw from another part of the zoo was brought in and placed near the tree trunks to complete their playground. Mr. Popplethwaite really wanted his new friends to be happy!

When the monkeys arrived at
the zoo, they looked tired and hungry.
Mr. Popplethwaite escorted them to
their new home. They were given plenty
of fresh fruit and water to help them
recover from their long journey
from the rainforest in Africa.

Mr. Popplethwaite then called a meeting of the zoos staff so he could tell them about the new arrivals. He also asked the zookeepers to help him come up with names for the monkeys. The youngest member of the staff, a stable boy named Tommy, excitedly spoke up and said he had names for them.

"Tell us." said Mr. Popplethwaite.

"Binky, Banky, and Bonky!" Tommy shouted.

Everybody liked his suggestion,
and all agreed they were great names.
From then on, Binky was the biggest,
Banky had a short tail
and Bonky was the smallest.

After a few days rest
and having settled in, the three little
monkeys appeared outside their new
home and began to explore. In no time
they were climbing up the ropes,
swinging on the tyre, and jumping
on and off the see-saw.
Mr. Popplethwaite was glad
to see the monkeys playing.

When the zoo opened
the next morning,
the visitors gathered around
and enjoyed watching
the monkeys play.

Binky, Banky, and Bonky
were very happy.
The three monkeys
had become best friends,
and all the staff agreed
they were a great addition
to the zoo.

(Catch them in their next
adventure when they help to feed
the other animals of the zoo.)

About the author of *The Adventures of Binky, Banky and Bonky*

George Bradley was born in Liverpool, England, in 1930. He was in
the Merchant Navy for several years. After leaving the service,
George received his degree as an engineering draughtsman.
He worked on nuclear submarines for several years before
becoming a technical consultant to various companies.

Today George resides in the town of Southport, England.
He is the father of three daughters
and eight grandchildren.

At age 90, George decided the next journey in his life would be
that of a published author, based on the children's stories
he has been telling his entire life.

Printed in Great Britain
by Amazon

79638814R00016